MISTLETOE AND MURDER

A Century Cottage Cozy Mysteries Novella

DIANNE ASCROFT

Marge Kirkwood gets more than she bargained for under the mistletoe at the Fenwater Association Christmas party: a bothersome blast from the past, and a murder to investigate. A nostalgic festive mystery set in small-town Canada in 1983.

MISTLETOE AND MURDER

≈ I ≈

"What the devil?" Marge Kirkwood almost gagged on the scent of Aqua Velva aftershave as strong arms trapped her in a vicelike bear hug.

Sometimes she wished she didn't have such a keen sense of smell. She thrust her arms outward, trying to free herself from the unexpected contact as she looked up to identify her assailant. Wet lips clamped onto hers before she could pull away.

"Merry Christmas, sweetheart!"

Marge barely resisted the urge to wipe her lips. "Just because it's Christmas doesn't mean you can grab me like that, Mike. What do you think you're doing?"

Mike Wilson pointed toward the ceiling and Marge groaned inwardly as she looked up. Another blasted sprig of mistletoe. She thought she knew where all of them were. She had checked the bar and lounge carefully when she arrived and had been ducking quickly through doorways to avoid unwanted gropes. But she hadn't spotted this one hanging from the chandelier in the middle of the main hotel foyer.

"What are you doing here?" Marge spat out.

Mike gave her the confident smirk that she remembered too well. "Don't look so surprised. Or pretend you're not glad to see me. I'm still a member of the Fenwater Association."

Marge raised her eyebrows. "But you closed your dad's hardware shop."

"Just ended the lease on the building. I didn't sell my stock. I'm gonna rent a place on St Andrew's Street. I couldn't get a better location than the main street. You should partner with me. We could work closely together." Mike gave her a suggestive wink.

Marge couldn't help thinking of the Aqua Velva slogan 'there's something about an Aqua Velva man'. Well, there was nothing appealing about this one.

"Not a chance, mister." Marge managed to choke out the words, keeping her tone level.

She knew she should at least be polite since this was the local business association's annual Christmas party, but Mike Wilson was the one person she had been happiest to leave behind after high school. All through their school years he never got the hint that she wasn't interested in him even when she started dating Ted Kirkwood in their last year of school.

"We haven't had a chance to catch up since you moved back to Fenwater. Let's get together for a drink," Mike said.

Marge fought to keep her expression neutral as she scanned the foyer for an excuse to escape. Ignoring Mike's invitation, she exclaimed, "Oh, there's Lois. I was looking for her."

Before Mike could reply, Marge made a beeline for her friend Lois Stone. After a quick hello to Lois's escort, Bruce Murray, Marge drew Lois aside. "Am I glad to see you!"

Lois raised her eyebrows. "What's got you so rattled? You're usually in your element at a party."

"Mike Wilson's driving me nuts. He's had a crush on me since high school and won't stop pestering me tonight."

"Is that the guy you were kissing under the mistletoe just now?"

"I wasn't kissing him! He grabbed me. I didn't even see that blasted bit of mistletoe there."

Lois grinned mischievously. "Isn't it the season for memorable moments under the mistletoe?"

"For you and Bruce, yeah. But not for me and Mike, no way."

Lois grinned. "You might have other options. Mike's not your only admirer tonight."

Oh, maybe this evening will get better, Marge thought. She pulled her shoulders back and stuck out her ample bust. Flipping her dyed-blonde hair out of her eyes, she batted her eyelashes coquettishly. "What can I say? I'm a flame that draws those moths." She narrowed her eyes at Lois. "So, who's interested?"

Lois kept her expression neutral. "Your ex."

"What!"

A laugh burst from Lois. "Yeah, when you two were in that clinch under the mistletoe, across the room I saw Ted glaring at Mike."

Marge scrunched up her face. "Yeah, Ted can't stand Mike 'cause he never got the message to scram once Ted and I started dating. But we've been split up for years. He shouldn't care now."

"I know Ted was a jerk when you were married and you were glad to split up with him, but he certainly looked jealous just now."

Marge really didn't want to think about her ex-husband possibly still having feelings for her. She shuddered. "Let's not even go there. Looks like I better tag along with you and Bruce tonight for protection." She grinned at Bruce. "As long as I'm not cramping your style."

Bruce gave Marge one of his easy smiles. "Not at all. I'll have Lois all to myself after the party."

Lois nudged her. "Actually, you'll be an asset. You know everyone so you can introduce me."

Bruce squeezed Lois's hand where it rested on his arm. "Absolutely."

Marge shifted position to stand beside Lois. From their vantage point near the entrance, Marge surveyed the festively decorated foyer. Hawick Hotel certainly had gone to a lot of effort. Strings of silver and green tinsel were entwined and draped over the pictures hanging on the walls. The shiny decorations complemented the deep green floral-patterned wallpaper. Holly garlands bedecked with red ribbons hung from the mahogany reception desk and even the clock behind the desk was ringed with a festive wreath. A huge Christmas tree stood in the corner beside the desk. The other end of the desk was transformed into a mini-bar with glasses of rum and eggnog, and hot whiskeys set out in neat rows.

Local businesspeople milled around the foyer, mingling and chatting. Marge spotted antique stall owner Dave Stewart in his red tartan kilt serving drinks at the mini-bar while chatting with Dean Walker, a fellow market trader.

As Marge noted how Dave's brightly patterned garment added to the festive mood, the market trader glanced across the room and met her gaze. She raised her hand in greeting and Dave smiled. He turned to speak to Dean then left the other man at the mini-bar and headed toward Marge and her companions.

As he approached, Marge said, "This is a change from helping at civic events. You're fixing something stronger than tea and coffee tonight. We'll have to find out what kind of bartender you are."

Dave laughed. "Oh, I'm not mixing the drinks, just serving. The hotel staff are whipping up the rum and eggnogs, and hot whiskies. And both of them are good."

Marge chuckled. "And how would you know that?"

Dave turned an innocent gaze on her. "Someone has to be responsible for quality control."

Marge raised one eyebrow, skeptically. "Not that you would volunteer, of course."

Her expression quickly deteriorated into a frown as Mike appeared and stepped between Marge and Dave. Marge edged closer to Lois on her other side. *Why couldn't this guy go and bother someone else tonight?*

"Howdy, everyone!" Mike said jovially. He narrowed his eyes at Dave and raised his nearly empty glass. "Hey, shouldn't you be at the bar? I'm almost ready for another."

"Never fear. Several Fenwater Association committee members are manning the mini-bar. You won't go without."

Mike grinned broadly and put his arm around Marge's shoulders. "That's what I like to hear. Great party, isn't it? And even better since I ran into my old buddy Marge."

Marge squirmed under Mike's embrace, trying to subtly shake him free, but his grip was firm.

"Making new friends, I see," a woman said sarcastically behind them.

Marge craned her neck to look over her shoulder. A tall, broad-shouldered woman standing behind her glared at Mike. Marge had heard Helen Young and Mike had split up recently. From the looks of it, they weren't on good terms.

Mike squeezed Marge's shoulder. "Nah, me and Marge go way back."

"We knew each other in high school. But not that well," Marge ground out.

Marge took a deep breath and tried to appear unconcerned as Helen turned her hostile gaze on her. She did not want to get in the middle of anyone's romantic troubles, nor did she want Helen to get the wrong idea about her and Mike. *Why couldn't Mike just clear off?*

"Well, I hope you enjoy rekindling your *friendship*," Helen snapped.

The woman turned and stomped away, pushing roughly through the crowd toward the mini-bar. Marge sighed, watching Helen's retreating figure. She didn't know the woman well, but she didn't want to make an enemy needlessly.

Marge's gaze was drawn away from Helen by a smaller woman in a cream knit top and black velvet skirt who stopped where Helen had just stood, a glass of eggnog cupped in both hands. The woman caught Marge's gaze and rolled her eyes, shaking her head slowly.

Marge raised her eyebrows in response and huffed out a breath to conceal her annoyance. Why did Sue Howard have to overhear the conversation? She wasn't afraid to give people something to talk about, but only if there was a grain of truth to it.

"Hi, Sue! Are you enjoying the party?"

"Yeah, it's even better than last year."

Marge pointed to the other woman's top. "Nice! Definitely your colour."

Smiling, Sue indicated Marge's red cocktail-length chiffon dress. "Thanks. Gorgeous dress."

Marge nodded her thanks then peered more closely at Sue's top. She motioned to a spot just above the waist. "You spill something?"

Sue glanced down and her face coloured. She vigorously brushed at the smudge of beige powder clinging to her top. "I'm such a klutz! I must have dropped foundation powder on it. I never even noticed it before I left the house."

Marge squinted at the top. "You got it. I can't see it now."

"Good, but I'd better go and sponge it. See you later!"

"Do you want me to hold your glass 'till you come back?"

Without answering, Sue gave a quick wave and disappeared.

Marge turned back to the group and tapped Lois's arm. "I'll have to introduce you to Sue later. Her fruit and vegetable stand in the market always has the freshest produce."

On her opposite side, Mike peered over his shoulder at the people surrounding the mini-bar. "Anyone see where Helen went? I don't want to run into her at the bar."

Dave stretched to look at the mini-bar. "She's not there."

Mike turned back to the group. "Good. Time for a refill. Anyone want anything?"

When no one spoke, Mike said, "Drinks for one then. Back in a minute."

As soon as Mike left, Marge whispered to Lois, "I hope not. I've had enough of him tonight. But I won't let him ruin my evening." She spoke to the group. "Okay, where's the food? I'm starving."

"They're setting out the buffet at seven o'clock. But there's potato chips and cookies," Dave said.

"Okay, I could devour some peanut cookies."

"Sorry, the choice is gingerbread, sugar cookies and shortbread," Dave replied.

"That'll do. Where are they?"

Dave motioned toward the lounge doorway. "Inside on the bar."

Marge scrunched up her eyebrows. "Funny, but I could have sworn I smelled cookies out here. Well, why don't Lois and I grab some nibbles for everyone?"

After a murmur of agreement from the group, Marge slipped her hand under Lois's elbow and nudged her toward the lounge, skirting the mistletoe hanging from the chandelier in the centre of the room. She wasn't taking any chances this time. From the corner of her eye, she saw a flash of movement as someone barrelled across the room. She turned her head to see who was in such a rush and immediately wished she hadn't. Of course, Mike was trying to catch up with her. It figured.

Still moving, Mike's gaze met hers and he held up his drink. "Have you tried the eggnog? Don't know what they've put in it but this glass is better than the last one."

"Not yet. We'll get some in a minute," Marge replied, edging toward the lounge.

If only she could make a run for it, but that was too obviously rude. With a couple of long strides, Mike caught up with the women. "Really, you've got to try some. Why don't I get you a glass?"

"Like I said, we'll get some soon."

As Marge spoke, she noticed that Mike was taking short, shallow breaths. She knew she could still turn heads but even she didn't have such a drastic effect on men. Good grief, he must be really out of shape. She would admit they weren't getting any younger, but a middle-aged man should be able to hurry across a room without being ready to collapse.

Mike wheezed, "Are you sure? I'd be glad to—"

"Thanks, but I'm starved." Marge turned back in the

direction of the lounge. "I need some sustenance before I get into the eggnog."

Ignoring her comment, Mike continued, his voice hoarse. "So good. Spice or something . . ."

Marge turned back to look at Mike. He was staring vacantly into his glass, swaying slightly.

She rested her hand on Mike's forearm. "You okay? Maybe you should ease up on the eggnog." Not receiving a response, she spoke louder, gently shaking him. "Mike! Are you alright?"

Mike looked at her then bent over, wheezing heavily. Marge slid her arm under his to support him, looking around for somewhere he could sit down. Suddenly Mike slumped to the ground, pulling Marge down on top of him and knocking the breath out of her. She quickly collected herself, pulling her arm out from under Mike and rising to her knees, heedless of the rip she heard in the chiffon fabric of her dress.

Marge peered into Mike's unconscious face then shouted, "Somebody find Doc McKinlay!"

She was aware of a flash of red as Dave Stewart knelt beside her.

"What happened to him?"

"He wasn't making much sense and just collapsed."

Marge gladly let Dave take over. He had first aid training and always knew what to do in a crisis. She crawled backwards to give him room, and Lois helped her to her feet. As she rose, her gaze fell on the damp patch under the mistletoe where Mike's drink was seeping into the thick red and gold carpet.

2

Marge flipped her hair back from her face, shivering in the stiff breeze. "I still can't believe Mike died. I mean, he bugged me and I tried to give him the slip at the party, but it's awful that he died." It had been two days since the party, and she hadn't wrapped her head around it yet.

"I know, and in such a tragic way," Lois agreed.

Marge picked up her pace, eager to reach the end of the block so she could get out of the cold. Several buildings ahead sat the square brick building they were heading for. Ontario Provincial Police officers used the local station as a base when patrolling the area.

Marge pulled the lapels of her red wool coat tighter around her neck. "At least the station is so small it'll be warm inside."

Lois thrust her hands deeply into the pockets of her dusty rose wool coat. "I wish we didn't have to go back to the police station. Not after our run-in with Constable Riley last fall."

"Try not to think about the fall fair. This is only a few

routine questions because Mike's death was unexpected. They must be talking to everyone who was at the party. We'll be out of there in no time."

"I sure hope so."

Marge bent her head against the breeze and plowed on.

"I can't believe the nerve of that broad!"

Marge looked up to see her ex-husband stomping toward them.

Ted stopped in front of the two women and glared at Marge. "She's not much older than our kids. The nerve of her!"

"Who?" Marge asked.

"That cop."

"Who, PJ?"

"Constable Ross. She doesn't like you calling her by her first name," Lois reminded her friend.

Marge gave a quick nod of acknowledgement then spoke to Ted. "So, you've been interviewed about Mike's death?"

"It was more like an inquisition."

Marge snorted, quirking up one side of her mouth. "Sure it was."

"I'm telling you, she wanted me to account for where I was the whole time I was at the hotel. And she asked why I had a grudge against Mike."

"Why would your history with Mike matter?"

"I don't know but she was acting like I was responsible for his death."

Marge shook her head. "That's ridiculous. Mike had a bad allergic reaction and they couldn't get him to the hospital in time." She regarded her ex-husband as he stared into the distance, his jaw clenched. "I'm sure Constable Ross isn't accusing you of anything. Lois and I are headed to the station now. I'll clear this up and call you later."

She'd mostly avoided her ex-husband after his recent move back to Fenwater, but she wasn't going to let her children's father be accused of murdering anyone.

Ted shrugged. "Well, I hope you have more luck with that broad than I did. Like I said, she's got it in for me."

Marge glared at Ted. "Don't go around badmouthing Constable Ross. That's not gonna do any good. I've known her since she was a kid and she's always fair. I'll get to the bottom of this."

Ted muttered, "I hope that'll be before I'm sitting in a jail cell."

Marge stifled her grunt of frustration. Ted had always tended to overreact. Hopefully his fears were unfounded this time. "Well, the kids will be home for Christmas in a couple weeks, and I don't intend to tell them their dad's been accused of murder so I'll get to the bottom of it alright."

After a quick goodbye, Marge strode even faster up the street. She heard Lois puffing beside her as she struggled to keep up. When they reached the police station, she turned to look at Lois. Noticing her friend's tense stance, she gave her a big grin. "We didn't get arrested the last time we were here so stop worrying. This isn't even about us."

Marge opened the door and stepped into the small utilitarian front office. Sitting at the battered wooden desk in the centre of the room, Constable Riley didn't look up. The two chairs that usually sat in front of his desk were missing. Instead, four straight-backed chairs were lined up under the front window.

Marge, with Lois trailing reluctantly behind her, strode to the police officer's desk. "Afternoon, Constable. I thought Constable Ross was interviewing people about Mike's death."

The officer glanced up at her then motioned to the

chairs under the window. "She is. Please take a seat, ladies, and she'll call each of you shortly."

Marge stared at the officer for a moment, surprised by his brusque manner. He couldn't have forgotten them in the couple of months since the fall fair. She gave Lois a puzzled look as they took their seats.

Marge rubbed her hands together, enjoying the heat in the room. "Better day in here than out there," she said to the officer.

When she got no response, she looked at Lois again and shrugged. Why was Constable Riley so uptight today? He was the new kid on the block last fall but he should be settling in now. Investigating unexpected deaths must be routine in police work. For this case, the officers just had to talk to the people who were at the party then they should be able to easily wrap up their enquiry.

A sandy-haired female officer opened the door of the back office and Dave Stewart stepped out. He greeted the women as he walked past them. "Nice to see you, ladies. I'd love to stop to chat but I left another trader watching my stall."

From the doorway to the back office, Constable Ross said, "Who's next, ladies?"

"Me." Marge turned to Lois and winked as she whispered, "I'll go first. Soften her up for you."

Marge chuckled at the look of alarm on her friend's face. She stood up and followed Constable Ross into the back office. The officer motioned to a chair in front of her desk and Marge sat down.

"I have a few questions about the party on Saturday night and Mike Wilson's death," Constable Ross said.

"Okay but I hope they won't be as strange as the ones you've been asking already."

The officer frowned at Marge. "The questions we're asking are pertinent to the enquiry."

"Then why ask people whether they had a grudge against Mike for an accidental death enquiry?"

Constable Ross silently regarded Marge.

"Isn't that going a bit too far?" Marge persisted. "You were born sensible and I don't think you've changed. So why are you going off on wild goose chases?"

Constable Ross narrowed her eyes. "This is a suspicious death enquiry."

"What? He had an allergic reaction. There must have been something at the hotel that he didn't know he was allergic to."

Constable Ross was shaking her head. "I got the preliminary autopsy report back this morning. They found a small fragment of peanut in his stomach contents."

"Peanuts! Even back in high school Mike was severely allergic to them. He wouldn't have eaten any ever. So how did he get it?"

"That's what we're trying to establish. So now I need you to tell me everything you can remember about the party."

Marge felt like she was in a daze as she recounted what happened at the party. Afterwards she returned to the outer office and motioned for Lois to go speak to Constable Ross, barely managing to give her friend a reassuring smile. She flopped onto a hardbacked chair.

The front door opening disturbed her revery. A well-dressed man walked in and sat down beside her.

"Hi, Marge. I guess I'm second in line?"

"No, you're next, Gary, I'm just waiting for my friend."

Judging by his smart, dark suit, Marge figured that Gary Hunter was on his way to work. Marge's eyebrows drew into a frown as she regarded the Hawick Hotel manager. Were his kitchen staff responsible for Mike's allergic reaction?

Marge sighed. "Mike's death is just terrible, and at the party of all places."

"Yes, it is. Our staff are very upset about it. They put so much work into the party and then a tragedy like that happens."

"Were you serving any food or drinks with peanuts in them?"

Gary shook his head. "Nope. I don't think we've ever made any drinks with peanuts. We didn't even start serving the buffet before the party ended, but none of the food had peanuts in it anyway."

"What about the snacks before the buffet?"

Gary narrowed his eyes at Marge. "Why all the questions about the food?"

"I've just heard that Mike died because of his peanut allergy."

Gary's eyes widened. "Oh, no! That's such a shame." He paused for a moment, staring at the floor. "I don't know how that happened but it definitely wasn't caused by the hotel. Like I said, all that we served before he died were snacks – potato chips and cookies. Definitely no peanuts in any of it."

Where did he get it then? Marge wondered.

Marge was jolted from her thoughts as Constable Ross called Gary Hunter into the back office. Lois re-joined Marge, looking more relaxed than she had before the interview.

Making an effort to paste a smile on her face, Marge said teasingly, "You aren't under arrest then?"

Lois chuckled, but glanced around her nervously. "No, but I was beginning to wonder if she suspected me of something with the questions she asked."

Marge patted and smoothed her hair. "Let's get out of here and I'll fill you in on what's happening. Fancy a drink?"

"Sure. The Honey Pot?"

"Not the diner today. I need something stronger than coffee."

❧ 3 ❧

Marge finished recounting her conversation with Constable Ross to Lois. She leaned back in the padded chair and sipped her whiskey, relishing the heat from the crackling fire in the small Rumford fireplace near their table. Dave Stewart was right. The Hawick Hotel made good hot whiskies. The traditional hotel was also a very comfortable place to unwind after her shock at what she'd learned at the police station.

She idly glanced toward the lounge doorway. Gary Hunter poked his head in, leaning his hand against the wide architrave as he surveyed the room. He smiled and nodded a greeting to the two women.

"Looks like the manager is back from his interview. I hope the hotel didn't make a mistake that caused Mike's death," Lois said.

"Yeah, and I hope the police don't get the wrong man. I'm gonna make sure they don't try to pin it on Ted. What a Christmas present that would be for the kids. He's pulled some stunts in his time but that would beat all, and it wouldn't even be his doing."

17

"Do you think someone slipped Mike the peanuts?"

"They must have. He would never have deliberately eaten them."

"Who would want to hurt him?"

"I guess that's what we need to figure out. My first thought is Helen, his ex-girlfriend. You saw the looks she was giving me, not to mention her snide comments. I don't know her well but we've seen she's the jealous type. I heard she moved to Fenwater about four years ago – before I came back from Toronto." Marge paused. "Helen often meets clients here. If we're lucky she'll stop by today."

"What does she do?" Lois asked.

"Interior designer. I heard she met Mike when he hired her to redecorate his house."

Lois frowned. "Are the police sure the hotel didn't accidentally serve something with peanuts in it at the party?"

Marge inclined her head toward the bar where the hotel manager was now talking to the barman. "I was chatting with Gary while you were in with Constable Ross and he's certain they didn't serve anything with peanuts in it."

As Marge watched the hotel manager, a tall woman in a tweed wool coat, trimmed with a fake fur collar, stepped into the lounge. She scanned the tables at the back of the room, hesitating briefly when she noticed Marge and Lois seated beside the fireplace. Without acknowledging them, the woman headed to a table on the opposite side of the room beside the window.

"Will you excuse me for a few minutes? I think I better speak to Helen on my own," Marge said.

Lois waved her away. "Go ahead. I'm fine here."

Marge rose and made her way to Helen before she had time to sit down. "I'm glad I caught you, Helen. I'd like to offer my condolences on your loss."

Helen regarded her coldly. "You know Mike and I weren't together when he died."

"Yes, but you had been going out until recently. I also wanted to clear the air between us. I think you got the wrong impression at the party."

"That you and Mike were hitting it off? I don't think so. You looked pretty cozy to me."

Marge shook her head slowly and took a deep breath, trying to keep her temper under control. "Sometimes looks can be deceiving. Mike was the one who was trying to get friendly. But I've known him since high school and I've never been interested in him. I was trying to get that through to him without making a scene."

The look Helen gave her dripped disbelief.

"I'm sure it wasn't easy seeing him looking at another woman when you hadn't split up that long ago, but for what it's worth, I didn't reciprocate his interest," Marge continued.

Helen gave a harsh laugh. "It doesn't matter. It just reminded me how he never could resist women."

"It sounds like he didn't treat you very well."

"Yeah, well, he put everything he had into wooing me when we first dated, but after a while his interest broadened, shall we say. Eventually I'd had enough of it."

"So you left him."

"Before I could dump him, he dumped me."

"Oh, that must have really stung," Marge said.

Helen narrowed her eyes. "True, but not enough to want him dead."

"You've heard that his death might be suspicious then?"

"Yeah, I've just come from the police station. But, like I said, his philandering annoyed me, and I guess I flew off the handle when I saw him with you at the party, but I wouldn't have tried to kill him. It just irked me to be reminded of what a low life he was. But, there's other fish in the sea, and I've got my business. I didn't need him."

Marge nodded. "You're probably one of the people who was closest to him lately though. So, if you didn't want to kill him, do you have any idea who else might?"

Helen pursed her lips as she gazed past Marge's shoulder toward the door. "My best guess would be Dean Walker."

"The shoe repair guy in the market?"

"Yeah, he loaned Mike money to upgrade shelving and other stuff for the shop he was opening, and I know Mike was avoiding him. He wouldn't set up a repayment schedule."

"But why would Dean want to kill Mike if he still owed him money?"

Helen shrugged. "I don't know. Maybe he just got fed up with the run around he was getting and snapped." Helen glanced toward the door again then turned to Marge. "Will you excuse me? There's my client."

Marge held out her hand. "Thanks for talking to me. I hope we've sorted things out and don't have any hard feelings."

Helen shook her hand. "None at all. Now I must go."

Helen went to meet her client as Marge returned to her table and sat down.

"How did it go?" Lois asked.

"Well, we've cleared the air." Marge quickly recapped the conversation for Lois.

"So, what do you make of it?"

"I don't know. I can't see why Dean Walker would kill Mike without getting the money he was owed. With an informal loan there may not be any paperwork to claim the money back from Mike's estate. And Helen says she's over Mike, but her feathers were certainly ruffled on Saturday night. I don't think we can completely discount her yet, but we also need to pay Dean a visit at the market tomorrow morning."

❄ 4 ❄

Marge cringed then mentally shook herself as she heard Perry Como singing over the loudspeaker about turkey and mistletoe making the season bright. Of course, she would be surrounded by all things Christmas in the market. It was the season to sell things after all. She scanned the overhead support beams for any sign of dangling greenery as she walked with Lois down the first aisle of the building. She wouldn't get caught out by mistletoe today.

Lois wore a huge grin. "The traders have their stalls decorated so beautifully. I love it!"

"I've no objection as long as they keep their mistletoe to themselves," Marge said.

Lois nudged her. "Don't be such a spoilsport. You never know, you might meet someone interesting under the mistletoe."

Marge narrowed her eyes at her friend. "Banish that thought. Just keep that stuff for you and your sweetheart. I'm giving it a wide berth." She stopped at a stall and turned to Lois, indicating wooden bins filled with an array of vegetables, including loose potatoes, carrots, Brussels sprouts and wax beans. "Aren't these amazing vegetables? You have to meet Sue. This is her stall."

Lois's eyes widened when she spotted a box of large ripe tomatoes. "Where does she get tomatoes like that at this time of year?"

The stallholder approached them, smiling. "I've got a heated greenhouse in my backyard so I grow all kinds of vegetables year round."

"Sue, have you met my friend Lois? She moved here last summer," Marge said.

Sue extended her hand to Lois, and the two women exchanged greetings.

Marge chuckled. "I bet Lois will be your best customer now. She loves fresh vegetables almost as much as apple and cinnamon muffins. And after the harvest next fall, she'll probably be around to stock up on apples for her baking."

Sue smiled. "Great. It's always good to have a new customer."

"While I'm here, can I get half a dozen tomatoes?" Lois asked.

"Sure." Sue picked out several juicy tomatoes and put them in a paper bag.

"Terrible about Mike, isn't it?" Marge said as she watched the stallholder.

Nodding, Sue took the money Lois handed her. "Must be awful to have an allergy like that."

"And even worse when someone used it to kill him," Marge replied.

"Yeah," Sue said.

Marge frowned. "Who would do such a thing?"

Sue quirked up the corner of her mouth and shook her head. "No idea. I hope they catch the guy."

Marge nodded agreement, then nudged Lois. "We better get on with our errands."

The two women walked on to the next aisle. Lois slowed as they passed a stall selling handknit garments. "Isn't that sweater gorgeous!"

Marge grinned. "And it just happens to be burgundy – your favourite colour." Marge inclined her head to indicate a stall on the opposite side of the aisle where a middle-aged man was tapping on the sole of a shoe with a small hammer. "There's Dean Walker's stall. We can come back here after we talk to him."

Marge crossed the aisle and stopped in front of the shoe repairman. "Working hard, Dean?"

Behind the counter, the man finished securing the sole of the shoe then looked up. "Yeah, flat out. With Christmas coming, everyone is rushing to get shoes repaired for parties."

Marge opened the flap on her large pink purse and pulled out a black velvet shoe bag. She pulled the drawstrings open and slid a pair of bright red sandals with three-inch stiletto heels onto the wooden counter.

"Can I add to your work? I need these reheeled for the museum staff party next week."

Dean lifted one of the shoes and studied the heel. "Yeah, that's no problem. I should have them ready in a couple of days."

"Great. Thanks. Speaking of parties, wasn't what happened Saturday night awful?"

Dean raised his eyebrows and huffed out a breath. "Yeah, it sure was."

"Did you talk to Mike during the evening?"

"Just to say hi. I hadn't been there too long when he collapsed. I was chatting with Dave Stewart at the mini-bar then I filled in for him for a few minutes so he could take a break. Then the party was over."

"So, you didn't spend any time with Mike?" Marge asked.

"No."

"Mike was talking to us then went to get a drink when you were on the bar. You didn't talk to him then?"

"No, it got busy on the bar so I didn't have time to talk to anyone. I didn't even notice him."

"You guys knew each other pretty well though," Marge said.

Dean shrugged. "Yeah, I guess. Everyone who has a business in town knows one another."

Marge frowned. "I thought you guys were buddies. Someone told me you helped him financially to set up his new shop."

"I did, but that was just helping a fellow businessman."

"That was good of you. It's a shame you probably won't get back what you lent him."

"Yeah, but there's no sense crying over spilled milk. I can't do anything about it."

"No, I guess not."

"But it's not the end of the world. I'm doing okay."

"I'm glad to hear it. Thanks again for fixing those shoes for me."

Marge and Lois said goodbye to the shoe repairman and walked down the aisle, stopping to have a quick look at the handknit garments stall.

Lois lifted the burgundy sweater then set it down and picked up a rose one. "Oh, I like them both. How can I decide? I better have a think about it."

As the two women walked back to the entrance of the building, Marge slowed and looked down the aisle nearest to the front doors then back at Lois. "Your tomatoes looked really good. I think I'll get a couple. Back in a sec."

Marge left Lois and headed to the vegetable stall. "Back again, Sue. I couldn't pass up the tomatoes. Would you give me three?"

Sue stooped to reach under the counter, which was set behind the bins of produce. A soft thud as she pulled out a small paper bag drew Marge's attention to the wooden floor behind the counter. A small bag of roasted mixed nuts had fallen from the shelf.

Sue lifted the bag of nuts, folded the top closed and set it under the counter again. "Thankfully, it didn't spill or I'd have nothing to snack on."

"I'm sure you need something to munch on when you're here all day," Marge said.

"Yeah. Otherwise, I'd be off to the bakery stall in the next aisle. Too many cakes won't help my weight."

"I'm waiting until after the Christmas festivities before I worry about mine," Marge said, laughing.

Sue put the tomatoes in a bag and took the coins Marge handed her. "It's a shame the Fenwater Association party took such an awful turn. Have you got any other parties coming up?"

"The museum's staff party next week. I just left my shoes with Dean Walker to get them reheeled."

"The party should be fun. Mmm, I guess Dean will be staying here now."

"Where was he going?" Marge asked.

"He was supposed to get space in Mike's new shop but I heard last week that Mike had changed his mind. Told Dean there wasn't room. He definitely won't be going anywhere now with Mike gone."

Marge tried to hide her surprise. "That's too bad for him."

Marge took her bag of tomatoes from Sue and went to meet Lois. As the two women stepped out of the market building, she turned to her friend. "I just heard something interesting."

"What?" Lois asked.

"Let's go across the road and grab a coffee and I'll tell you."

Marge strode toward the traffic lights and Lois half-skipped to catch up with her.

※ 5 ※

Marge cast an exasperated look at the sprig of mistletoe hanging inside the door of the Honey Pot diner. She was fed up with seeing them everywhere she turned. If Mike hadn't caught her under the mistletoe and kindled Ted's jealousy, she wouldn't be investigating his death.

She sighed loudly. *My bad luck, but I can't turn the clock back. Looks like I'll have to see this through.*

Marge took another breath and made an effort to smile as she met Lois's gaze across the table in the window booth. She cupped one hand around her steaming mug of coffee, waving her other hand to indicate the plates of muffins set in front of them. "I'm not thinking about healthy eating until well past Christmas. After gingerbread muffins are off the menu."

Lois took an appreciative sip of her coffee, murmuring agreement. "Uh huh, ginger and cinnamon together. Wonderful. Now tell me what Sue said that was so interesting."

"Well, before we went to see Dean, I found it hard to

believe that he had any reason to kill Mike. After all, Helen said Mike had borrowed money from him."

Lois nodded. "I know. He wouldn't get his money back if he killed Mike."

"Exactly. So, I'd pretty much ruled Dean out. His business is doing well and it looks like he could survive losing the money. But then Sue mentioned just now that Mike reneged on renting space in his new shop to Dean. I bet that made him mad."

Lois shrugged. "It must have been annoying but he still has his stall in the market. And, like you said, his business is thriving."

"Yes, but Mike's new shop was right on the main street. More people would see Dean's shoe repair there than where he is in the back aisle of the market. He lost a great opportunity. That might have been enough to make him angry."

"But angry enough to kill Mike?"

Marge cocked her head, considering the possibility. "Maybe. Or at least angry enough to want to make him ill. Maybe he didn't realize how severe Mike's peanut allergy was."

Lois nodded thoughtfully. "That could be."

"I know it doesn't all add up but I think he has to be considered."

"And what about Helen? You didn't sound like you completely believed her about being over Mike."

"I don't, no matter what she says. Not after her attitude Saturday night."

"So, there's Helen and Dean. Anyone else?" Lois asked.

Marge flipped her hair back from her face. "I've tried to avoid Mike since I moved back to Fenwater so I don't know much about his life now. He always had an eye for the ladies. I'll have to ask around and find out who else he's dated recently, and whether he's made any enemies for any reason."

"Like jealous husbands?"

"Possibly. That's a good point."

Marge glanced across the room to where the waitress was stacking clean glasses onto a shelf, her back turned to the room. "Josie!"

The waitress spun around and picked up the coffee pot. Slipping out from behind the counter, she headed over to the window booth. "You ladies need a refill?"

"Great, thanks, Josie." Marge watched the waitress refill their cups. "I didn't see you at the Fenwater Association party on Saturday. Thought you would have represented the Honey Pot."

"We didn't close until six. By the time I got changed and headed over, with what happened to Mike and all, the party had shut down."

"Mike's death was a terrible shock."

Josie nodded agreement.

"I don't think I've ever seen him in here," Marge said.

Josie set the glass coffee pot on the table. "He didn't sit in often. Usually stopped by for takeout coffees."

"On his own?"

"Used to be him and his dad on their way to the shop. Then just him after his dad retired."

"What have you heard about him? Did he have many girlfriends? Or any enemies?"

Josie put her hand on her hip. "Now, you know I don't go in for gossip, Marge."

"I know that. I'm only asking 'cause the police were grilling Ted about how he and Mike got along. They might not have liked each other, but Ted had nothing to do with Mike's death. I want to make sure the police have the whole picture."

Shaking her head, Josie looked at Marge. "I can't believe Ted would have done anything to hurt him. I don't know much about Mike though. He dated Helen Young recently, but I don't think they were still together when he died." Josie tapped her lips. "Mmm, who else did he date? Oh yeah, I heard he dated a couple of women from out of town and used to drive down to Guelph to see them."

"Whoever killed him must have been at the party, so it has to be someone local," Marge said. "A businessman he got on the wrong side of?"

"I never heard of him having any big feuds with anyone. Nothing anyone would want to kill him over."

Across the table Marge heard Lois humming softly. She stopped speaking and looked at her friend, becoming aware of the Christmas background music in the diner.

Lois started under the scrutiny and blushed. "Oh sorry, I love that Rudolph song. I didn't mean to hum out loud."

Josie laughed, ignoring Marge's mock scowl. "Every-one's getting into the holiday mood. Have you heard about the Christmas bake sale? The market is letting our church set up a table to sell cookies to raise money for charity. Would you two like to donate cookies to the sale?"

"Sure, I can bake a couple dozen. Just let me know what kind you want," Lois said.

Marge winked at Lois. "My talents lie elsewhere but I'll buy the ingredients if my good friend here will bake my batch."

Lois nodded. "Sure."

Marge laughed. "Make mine peanut cookies. I've had a hankering for them since the party. I could have sworn I smelled them Saturday night."

Lois shook her head. "I can't see how. We weren't even near the snacks and Dave said they didn't have peanut cookies."

Marge shrugged. "I know but I still think I smelled peanuts. So make mine peanut cookies."

Josie lifted the coffee pot from the table. "Thanks, ladies. We need all the cookies we can get for the charity sale." She started to move away but turned back again. "You're going to the Christmas Lights hayride tomorrow night, aren't you?"

"Hayride? Isn't that for kids? Our youth group had them when I was a teenager," Lois said.

Marge shook her head emphatically. "Nope, not around here. Townsfolk of all ages come. The market stays open late and they serve hot apple cider and gingerbread cookies after the hayride."

Lois laughed. "Let me guess, Dave Stewart organizes that."

Josie nodded. "Of course. Who else? The evening is lots of fun."

Marge winked. "And you'll have an excuse to cuddle up to your honey on the wagon. Come on, we should go."

Marge laughed when she saw the blush creeping up Lois's cheeks. Lois and Bruce were so cute together.

"Okay, I'll phone Bruce tonight and invite him," Lois said.

"Great. I'll see you two there tomorrow then." Josie crossed the room and set the coffee pot back on the burner then spun around. "Oh!"

Marge and Lois turned to look at Josie, waiting expectantly.

"I just remembered. I think Mike went out with Sue Howard four or five years ago. They dated for a few months."

"I never knew that. Was it a bad breakup?" Marge asked.

Josie quirked up one side of her mouth. "I never heard anything like that. I think it just ended."

"Thanks, Josie." Marge turned to Lois. "Interesting. Sue didn't sound like she knew Mike any better than any of the other businesspeople in town."

"Is that Sue at the vegetable stall?" Lois asked.

"Yup. We'll have to catch her when her guard is down and chat with her some more. Hopefully she'll be at the hayride. I'd like to know more about her relationship with Mike."

❧ 6 ❧

Lois snuggled against Bruce, her hand nestled under his elbow. "There's such a great atmosphere here tonight."

Marge chuckled, watching her friend's wide-eyed expression. "I told you everyone comes. Wait 'till you see the houses lit up. Our townsfolk go all out."

Lois's expression changed to dismay. "Oh, dear. My little electric candle wreaths in the windows probably won't measure up to the town's expectations."

Bruce squeezed her hand. "I can help you put up lights along your porch and roof if you want to."

Lois smiled. "Thanks. I might take you up on that. Marge sure is lucky with just a couple windows in her condo to decorate."

Marge laughed. "That's about all I can manage. And I do it without even the tiniest sprig of mistletoe."

"Marge, where's your Christmas spirit?" Bruce chided.

She gave him a mock glare. "I have it. I just focus on the important aspects of the holiday."

Lois smirked. "Like gingerbread muffins, hot whiskeys, and parties?"

The perfectly coiffed blonde patted her hair. "Nothing wrong with that."

Marge swivelled so that she stood beside Lois, and scanned the crowd milling around outside the wooden market building. Children darted in and out among the adults, yelling and chasing each other, but stopped to stare when six flatbed wagons pulled by pairs of muscular draft horses stopped on the road in front of the building.

"How will they ever fit everyone on those wagons?" Lois asked.

"Some people like to walk the route. It's only a few blocks. There'll be enough seats for everyone who wants to ride," Bruce replied.

Marge hoped Sue would be here tonight. She needed to ask her a few questions.

Bruce bowed and swept his hand toward the wagons. "Our carriage awaits, ladies."

Despite Bruce's encouragement, Marge didn't budge. She thought quickly to find an excuse for stalling. "Let the crowd thin a bit then we'll pick a wagon."

Marge scanned the crowd until she spotted a short woman wearing jeans and a turquoise ski jacket with a pink hat and matching gloves. "Oh, there's Sue. It looks like she's on her own. Let's join her," she said quickly.

Without waiting for her friends to reply, Marge barrelled toward the woman. "Hi, Sue! Won't this be fun?" She motioned toward one of the wagons that was nearly empty. "I like the look of those big grey guys. Let's take that one."

Marge urged Sue toward the wagon, not giving her a chance to refuse. Behind her, she heard the footsteps of Lois and Bruce crunching on the snow and knew they were following her. When they reached the open-sided wagon, Marge asked Bruce to help the women climb aboard. He offered his hand and steadied Sue as she mounted the movable wooden steps set beside it.

Before Marge could follow her, Helen appeared from the opposite side of the wagon and started up the steps. "Sue, I'm glad I spotted you! I've got some ideas for your bedroom revamp."

Lumbering up the steps in Helen's wake, Marge damped down a huff of annoyance as she watched Helen settle beside Sue on the near side of the double row of hay bales. She plumped down next to Helen, taking a deep breath to calm down. Lois and Bruce climbed on and took seats on hay bales facing the opposite side of the wagon with their backs to the women.

When all the seats were filled, the driver flicked the reins and called to the horses. Making a sharp creaking sound, the wagon jerked forward. After several steps the horses settled into a smooth stride.

Marge leaned forward to speak to Helen and Sue, focusing her gaze on Sue. "I haven't done this in years – not since before I moved to Toronto. When were you last on a Christmas Lights hayride?"

Sue shrugged. "I come along some years."

Marge glanced at Helen. Although she wanted to talk to Sue, she couldn't ignore Helen sitting between them.

Helen glanced away then back at the other two women. "Mike and I came last year," she said softly.

Marge heard the sadness in her voice. No matter how much Helen protested that she no longer cared about Mike after the couple's breakup, it was obvious that wasn't true. Marge felt sympathy for the woman, but she couldn't help wondering what was the balance between sadness and anger in Helen's feelings for her ex-boyfriend.

Out of the corner of her eye, Marge noticed that Dean Walker was sitting next to Lois and Bruce. Dean's wife sat primly beside her husband.

Marge twisted her upper body and leaned across to speak to Lois. "You two comfy over there?"

Lois leaned against Bruce as he slipped his arm around her shoulder. "Yes, thanks."

Marge turned her attention to the shoe repairman. "Oh, hi, Dean. You having a night off from the holiday season repair rush?"

"Yeah, my wife loves the hayride, but don't worry. Your shoes will be ready for your party." Dean reached for his wife's hand and held it loosely in both of his as he turned to smile at her.

Before Marge could try to regain Dean's attention, the wagon jolted as the horses made a sharp right turn onto a residential street. Marge gripped the edge of the bale she was seated on and rolled with the motion of the vehicle. Behind her, she heard Lois's exclamations of awe and knew her friend had spotted the decorations on the houses they were now passing

"Oh, look at that house. All blue lights. It's so beautiful with the snow on the lawn!" Lois said.

"Didn't I tell you?"

Despite her comment, Marge was also impressed. Driving to work each day, she didn't pay much attention to her surroundings. This was the first time she had noticed the Christmas decorations in the neighbourhood. The bright, twinkling lights on the houses really were pretty. A house several doors further on caught her eye. It was deco-rated completely in red and white lights that flashed in ever-changing patterns. She loved it.

Marge turned her attention back to Dean, leaning closer to speak to him privately. "It's a shame Mike didn't have space for you in his new shop."

As Dean turned to look at her, she watched carefully for his reaction to her comment but he didn't seem perturbed by it.

Dean gave her a nonchalant shrug. "It didn't matter really. And it's just as well I never made any arrangements with him since there won't be a shop now. I'm glad that was my second choice."

Marge was aware of Dean's wife turning to look at her. The other woman didn't say anything but her eyes narrowed. Marge would have to keep this conversation short so the woman didn't get the wrong idea.

"What do you mean?" Marge asked.

"I had another offer. Canada Hardware has space to set up shop with them. I'm moving there after Christmas."

Marge's eyes widened but she pasted a big smile on her face. "Oh, that's great."

She wasn't sure which she was most surprised about: that Dean's motive for murder had just evaporated or that the shoe repairman would soon be working at the same premises as her ex-husband. Since she was trying to avoid Ted as much as possible, maybe she should find a new shoe repairman. She sighed. It seemed she was at a dead end with Dean. Time to learn more about Sue and maybe Helen.

Marge listened to Lois exclaim over another outstandingly illuminated house they passed and murmured agreement then turned back to her side of the wagon. She leaned toward Helen to join the women's conversation.

"I'm having a man-free Christmas," Helen said.

Sue laughed. "Tending my greenhouse plants keeps me busy. I don't have time for men."

"Make that three of us. I'm firmly single too." Marge took a deep breath. It was time to see if she could ruffle a few feathers to learn a bit more about her companions. "I guess dating Mike has put you both on your guard."

In the ensuing silence, Helen and Sue looked at each other. Marge waited.

"You dated Mike?" Helen asked Sue.

"Yeah, several years ago. Just for a few months."

Helen clasped her mittened hands together on her lap. "Not that it matters to me, but I didn't know."

"It was before you moved to Fenwater. I'd pretty much forgotten about it." Sue's gaze slid away from Helen.

"Mike was a hard guy to forget easily," Marge observed.

Sue rested her hands on the edge of the bale and leaned forward to look directly at Marge. The pitch of her voice rose. "Like I said, it was ages ago. Both of us moved on with no hard feelings."

"Just like Mike and me," Helen said quickly.

The conversation turned from the women's plans for Christmas to other topics, but there were awkward pauses and Marge often had to ask questions to keep it going. She watched each of the women closely, trying to gauge what thoughts and emotions might be churning inside them.

Beside Sue, two teenage boys were wrestling over a chocolate bar held by the one nearest to her. Leaning forward on the bale to avoid their elbows, Sue gave the boys a sharp look then turned back to the other women.

The boys were still for a moment, then the boy furthest from Sue made a lunge for the candy. He missed it but shoved his friend hard against Sue's hunched form. Marge gasped as Sue tumbled forward and fell from the wagon. She hit the ground with a thump.

Without hesitation, Marge slid off the hay bale and slithered to the edge of the wagon bed, letting her legs dangle over the side. Helen leaned forward as if she planned to follow her.

"It's okay. I'll go. We'll catch up with you," Marge called to Helen.

7

M arge leaned backwards, letting her heavier top half anchor her as she slid awkwardly from the wagon. She held her breath and hoped her feet would land first. The breath she was holding whooshed out when she felt the ground beneath her boots. As she hurried toward Sue, she saw an event marshal heading in the same direction. Sue was struggling to her feet as the pair reached her.

Marge offered her arm for support. "You okay?"

Sue's voice was shaky. "I think so."

"You're lucky you didn't break anything," the marshal said. "We better get you checked at the hospital."

Marge turned at the sound of the familiar voice. "Ted!"

In her rush to get to Sue, Marge hadn't looked at the marshal until he spoke. Her ex-husband nodded a greeting then turned his attention back to Sue.

"I'll call one of the guys to come and pick you up." Ted raised his walkie-talkie to his mouth.

Sue shook her head. "No, I don't need to go to hospital. Just my foot's a bit sore. It'll be okay if I walk on it."

Marge glanced around them for somewhere Sue could

rest. Pointing at a fence on a nearby property, she said, "Let's get her over there."

Marge and Ted each gripped one of Sue's arms and helped her hobble to the fence. Sue huffed out a breath and sank against it.

"Let me take a look at your leg," Ted said.

"Okay."

Ted ran his hand down the lower half of Sue's leg and gently flexed her foot. "Does that hurt? Are you sore anywhere else?"

"No, like I said, just my foot. It'll be fine in a few minutes."

Ted straightened up and Sue pushed off from the fence. She gingerly limped back and forth, testing her foot as the trio watched the rest of the wagons pass them. After several minutes, the last wagon had disappeared into the darkness and the sound of harnesses jingling grew fainter.

"When you ladies are ready, we can cut across a couple of blocks to catch up with your wagon. Or I can get someone to pick you up and take you back to the market. Your choice," Ted said.

Sue stopped pacing. "Maybe a ride to the market. I don't know how I'd climb onto the wagon again."

"That sounds best." Marge doubted that she would be able to jump onto a moving wagon either. Without the steps, she would be like a whale hauling herself onto the beach. Waiting for their ride would also give her time alone with Sue. She still had questions for her.

Ted pressed the button on his walkie-talkie to speak to the event organizers then turned to the women. "Dave Stewart will be over in a few minutes." He addressed Sue, "By the way, we've got the mortars and pestles you were looking for in the store now. Want me to put a set aside for you?"

"Ah, no. Th-that's okay," Sue stuttered. "I got one."

"No problem. Well, I should get back to my duties. Are you ladies okay here until Dave picks you up?"

"Yeah, we'll walk a bit until he arrives," Sue said.

After Ted said goodbye and strode off, Marge and Sue slowly made their way toward St Andrew's Street two blocks away.

"Why do you need a mortar and pestle?" Marge asked.

"For baking."

Marge chuckled. "You're more talented than me. I can't bake to save my life. What are you baking?"

"Cookies for Christmas gifts."

"Sounds good. I've been hankering for peanut cookies this week for some reason."

Sue winced as she took a step. "Oh, I made some of those."

"Do you crush the peanuts?"

Sue gave Marge an uneasy look then glanced away. "Uh huh, I don't like them crunchy."

"Lois uses peanut butter. Less hassle she says."

Sue shrugged. "Yeah, I guess."

Marge noticed that the lights ahead on the main street were little more than a block away. She needed to take advantage of the time she had left alone with Sue.

"So, you and Mike used to date, eh?" Marge said.

"Yeah, like I said, it was ages ago."

"I think Helen was surprised to hear that."

"It shouldn't matter to her. I'd never have gone out with him again."

"Why not?" Marge asked.

"He was such a Casanova."

Marge nodded. "Yeah, he always did go after what he wanted."

"You can say that again," Sue muttered, a hard edge creeping into her voice.

Marge had to strain to hear her comment. "What?"

Sue waved her hand dismissively. "Ah, nothing important."

Marge looked at Sue. The other woman's fingers were curled tensely and her jaw was tight. Sue's foot must be more painful than she let on. Maybe she should ease up on her. It sounded like Sue and Mike were ancient history. What reason would she have to kill him now?

Marge sighed. It looked like she could cross Sue off her suspect list. So that only left Helen unless she could find anyone else who had a grudge against Mike. When the wagons returned to the market, she would ask Helen a few more questions.

Marge changed the topic. "Have you got much more baking to do for Christmas?"

"Nah, I've got most of it done."

"You must have started early."

"No, only last week."

"After you got your mortar and pestle."

There was a short silence. "Uh, yeah."

As the women walked, Marge thought about the previous Saturday evening, picturing Sue in her cream top. It was right after she talked to Sue that she could have sworn she smelled peanut cookies. Marge had to stifle a gasp as a sudden realization hit her. Was that powder on Sue's top really makeup foundation? Could it have been powdered peanuts? Sue had the mortar and pestle by then. And she skittered away after Marge mentioned the powder on her clothes, supposedly to clean her top. She would have passed the mini-bar on the way to the ladies' restroom. Did she add peanuts to a drink then? But it didn't make sense. Why would she do it?

Marge turned to Sue and found the other woman staring back intently. Marge quickly broke eye contact with her, trying to hide the disturbing thoughts that were going through her head.

Smoothing her red ski jacket with both hands, she tried to sound upbeat. "Good thing it's not too cold tonight since I've only got my short jacket. I hope our ride gets here soon. We don't want to walk right to the other end of St Andrews Street."

"I need a break." Sue stopped walking abruptly. "Why were you looking at me like that?"

"Like what?"

"Like you were shocked."

"No, I wasn't. What gave you that idea?"

Sue leaned toward Marge, her leather barrel purse gripped tightly in one hand. "Why all the questions about Mike?"

Marge laughed, nervously. "Just curious."

Marge didn't expect the blow and staggered backwards onto the snow-covered lawn beside them, clutching her pounding head. Sue dropped her purse then jumped on her, punching wildly. Marge automatically raised her arms to block the blows.

"Why did you have to ask so many questions!" Sue screamed.

Stopping a blow aimed at her head, Marge caught Sue's arm and held it tightly. Sue's crazed, determined look scared her.

Marge ground out, "They know we're together. If you do anything to me, everyone will know it was you."

Panting, Sue tried to twist away from her. "I'll tell them you slipped on the ice. Hit your head."

Sue struggled, trying to free her arm from Marge's grip, but Marge used her larger size and weight to tip Sue from her. She flipped the pair of them to put herself on top of the smaller woman, hoping she wouldn't succumb to her dizziness and could restrain Sue until their ride arrived.

Marge held on grimly and was relieved when she heard a car's engine. The vehicle was moving slowly along the street toward them. Silently, she urged Dave to quickly spot them and come to her aid. As if the driver had heard her thoughts, the car increased its speed. It stopped at the curb. Car doors clicked open then two police officers were beside them, pulling the women apart.

Constable Riley tugged Marge's arm. "Break it up, ladies."

Marge let go of Sue and stood up, her vision blurry as she watched the other officer help Sue to her feet. "I'm glad to see you, PJ, uh . . . Constable Ross. I think Sue murdered Mike. I might have been next."

Constable Ross tightened her grip on Sue's arm.

"She's lying," Sue screamed.

"You know I'm not."

"Let's go to the station, ladies. Constable Riley, will you ride in the back with Sue?"

Constable Ross steered Sue toward the police cruiser. Sue gave Marge a hate-filled glare over her shoulder.

Her head fuzzy, Marge tried to make sense of what she had discovered. "Why, Sue? Revenge? Jealousy? Did you still want him?"

Sue spit out her reply. "No, I didn't want that jerk. But I had no hope of competing with him."

Marge frowned. "What?"

"We'll finish this at the station, ladies. Marge, you ride up front with me," Constable Ross said.

Marge made an effort to smile even though her head ached. "Sure thing. Will you let Dave Stewart know we got a better offer and won't need a ride now?"

8

"Sorry I couldn't meet you earlier but I couldn't skip band practice. Our pipe band has lots of engagements coming up for the holiday season," Lois said.

Marge took a sip of her hot whiskey and leaned back in her chair. "It's me who should apologize for just disappearing on you like that last night."

Lois waved her hand dismissively. "Don't give it another thought. Dave Stewart told us where you were and you've explained what happened. It's lucky the police patrol spotted you 'cause Dave got delayed going to pick you up."

Marge glanced around the room, noticing several of Lois's bandmates standing near the short mahogany bar at the front of the Hawick Hotel lounge. "It was lucky alright. Did you manage to enjoy the rest of the tour without me?"

Lois smiled. "Bruce and I had a good time. But I missed you and you missed the hot apple cider."

"But you missed all the excitement. Things happened pretty fast."

Concern wrinkled Lois's brow as she looked at her friend. "I'm really sorry I wasn't there with you. When you went to help Sue, I never imagined that you would be alone with a killer."

Marge shook her head. "Neither did I. Even though I was asking questions, I didn't actually think it was Sue. Boy, was I glad PJ spotted us."

"You said Sue killed Mike over his shop?"

"Yeah, after we got to the police station she got really upset. I didn't have to be in the back room with them to hear her. That shop is a guaranteed money-earner on the main street. When it became vacant, Sue and Mike both wanted to rent the premises. Sue does well in the market but she would do even better on St Andrew's Street where people could park outside and nip in. She was really angry that Mike offered to pay a higher rent than she could afford. I guess it didn't help that he was such an idiot to her when they dated too."

"Well, now neither of them will get that shop. Her business will go down the drain and who knows how long she'll spend in jail." Lois frowned. "She seemed nice. I would never have guessed she could kill someone. How did she get Mike to eat the peanuts?"

"Earlier in the evening, she got a glass of eggnog from the bar. No one paid any attention to her sitting at one of the tables at the back of the lounge. When no one was looking, she added powdered peanuts from a small container she had ready in her purse. Then she just had to carry the drink around until she found Mike."

"And you realized that the powder on her top was peanuts because the smell made you think of peanut cookies."

"Exactly. After I talked to her, instead of going to the restroom like she said she was, she headed to the bar and intercepted Mike when he went to get a refill. After she gave him the drink with the peanuts in it, she made an excuse and left him. No one saw her give Mike the drink or remembered seeing them together. Of course, she never mentioned to the police that she even spoke to Mike at the party."

"So, if you hadn't figured out that she had peanut powder on her top, it might have taken the police ages before they considered her. You were so clever!"

Marge huffed out a breath. "And scared. To be honest, I wish I hadn't confronted her on my own. I don't know what she had in her purse but I still have a headache from the clout she gave me. No concussion, thankfully. I prefer it when we do our snooping as a duo."

"There's definitely safety in numbers," Lois agreed.

A cough beside the table drew the attention of both women.

"Snooping? I thought you ladies were giving up on that? Look at all the scrapes you've landed in when you poked around in police matters." Bruce gave the two women a reproving look as he pulled out a chair and sat down beside Lois, wrapping his arm around her shoulder.

Marge finished her whiskey, reached for the brown leather handles on her large pink bag and stood up. "I think I'll leave you two to discuss that. I'm heading home to have an early night." She winked. "Make the most of the season, you two. There's mistletoe everywhere in this place."

After a quick round of goodbyes, Marge left Lois and Bruce and crossed the lounge. She waved and called goodnight to several people standing near the bar but didn't stop to talk. Her fire-red Skylark Buick was parked out front and it was only a short drive home. She would be able to kick off her shoes and fall onto her sofa in no time.

At the doorway, she came face to face with Ted entering the lounge. Before she could react, he clasped her shoulders and leaned in to kiss her. She pulled away from the kiss, glaring.

Ted pointed to the doorframe above. "Mistletoe."

Oh, blast, Marge thought. *I forgot all about that one.* "Don't you go getting any ideas. I divorced you for good reason."

Ted held his hands up in a placating manner. "I know. I'm not trying to rekindle us. That's a thank you for figuring out who killed Mike so I won't spend Christmas in the slammer."

"Well, uh, you're welcome. I couldn't let you ruin the kids' Christmas." She fixed him with a hard stare. "So don't get into any other trouble in the next week or so."

Ted gave a mock salute. "No, ma'am."

Marge left Ted and crossed the foyer, giving the mistletoe hanging from the chandelier a wide berth. She moved with her usual confident flounce, but she felt the tiredness seeping in. She had had more than enough mistletoe and murder this Christmas.

NEWSLETTER

To learn about the latest stories and novels in the *Century Cottage Cozy Mysteries* series, and the author's other books, please sign up to receive **Dianne Ascroft's newsletter**: https://landing.mailerlite.com/webforms/landing/y1k5c3

All information supplied will be kept private and will not be shared.

A Timeless Celebration
A Century Cottage Cozy Mystery Book 1

When an artefact from the Titanic is stolen before her town's 150th anniversary celebration, it's up to Lois Stone to catch the thief.

Middle-aged widow Lois has moved from bustling Toronto to tranquil Fenwater and is settling into her new life, feeling secure away from the dangers of the city. Then three events happen that shatter her serenity: her house is burgled twice and an antique watch belonging to a Titanic survivor is stolen from the local museum. Her best friend, Marge was responsible for the watch's safekeeping until its official presentation to the museum at the town's 150th anniversary party and its disappearance will jeopardise her job. Lois won't let her friend's reputation be tarnished or her job endangered by an accusation of theft. She's determined to find the watch in time to save her best friend's job and the town's 150th anniversary celebration.

And so begins a week of new friends, apple and cinnamon muffins, calico cats, midnight intruders, shadowy caprine companions and more than one person with a reason to steal the watch, set against the backdrop of century houses on leafy residential streets, the swirling melodies of bagpipes, a shimmering heat haze and the burble of cool water. *A Timeless Celebration* is the story of Lois's unwitting entry into the world of amateur sleuthing in a small town which beckons readers to stop and stay a while.

The novel is available on Amazon in paperback and e-book. For details, visit Dianne's Amazon page:

Amazon US: https://www.amazon.com/Dianne-Ascroft/e/B002BOCBKA

Amazon UK: https://www.amazon.co.uk/Dianne-Ascroft/e/B002BOCBKA

CENTURY COTTAGE COZY MYSTERIES

THE *Heritage Heist*

DIANNE ASCROFT

The Heritage Heist
A Century Cottage Cozy Mystery Book 2

A fall fair, a cornered craftsman, an heirloom heist. When an antique quilt that is a cherished part of Fenwater's past disappears from the market before her town's fall fair, it's up to Lois to resolve the quilt quandary.

Middle-aged widow Lois is enjoying her second season in her new town and her century house, away from the dangers of big city life in Toronto. She can't wait to experience her first old-fashioned fall fair, complete with hot apple cider. But when the local market is burgled, her enthusiasm for the upcoming festival plummets. During the break-in one of the security guards is badly injured and an antique quilt, on loan from the museum, vanishes. Her friend, Bruce, designed and built the display case and has one of only two keys to secure it. That makes him a prime suspect in the theft. Lois won't let Bruce's reputation, nor the trust his customers have in the bespoke furnituremaker, be damaged by the allegation. She's determined to piece the clues together to find the quilt, clear Bruce's name and save a piece of Fenwater's history.

And so begins a week of deepening friendships, hot apple cider, calico cats, backseat shenanigans, hazy housemates, and few puzzle pieces to work with, set against the backdrop of a rustic market building amidst stately stone architecture, the crackle of flames in the hearth, a blaze of colour on leafy residential streets and the scintillating scent of cinnamon.

The novel is available on Amazon in paperback and e-book. For details, visit Dianne's Amazon page:

Amazon US: https://www.amazon.com/Dianne-Ascroft/e/B002BOCBKA

Amazon UK: https://www.amazon.co.uk/Dianne-Ascroft/e/B002BOCBKA

ABOUT THE AUTHOR

Dianne Ascroft is a Canadian who has settled in rural Northern Ireland. She and her husband live on a small farm with an assortment of strong-willed animals.

She is currently writing the Century Cottage Cozy Mysteries series.

Her previous fiction works include *The Yankee Years* series of novels and short reads, set in Northern Ireland during the Second World War; *An Unbidden Visitor* (a tale inspired by Fermanagh's famous Coonian ghost); *Dancing Shadows, Tramping Hooves: A Collection of Short Stories* (contemporary tales), and an historical novel, *Hitler and Mars Bars*, which explores Operation Shamrock, a little known Irish Red Cross humanitarian endeavour.

Dianne writes both fiction and non-fiction. Her articles and short stories have been printed in Canadian and Irish magazines and newspapers.

For more information about the author and her books, visit

her website:
www.dianneascroft.com
her Facebook page:
www.facebook.com/DianneAscroftwriter
Twitter:
@DianneAscroft
Sign up for her newsletter:
landing.mailerlite.com/webforms/landing/y1k5c3

Printed in Great Britain
by Amazon

33180470R00037